HER
TESTIMONY

INSPIRED BY TRUE EVENTS

RIBHA

Waiting on God's timing is hard. His timeline is almost never aligned with the one we desire. Yet, His timing is always perfect - even though it can be hard to wait for.

If you're in a season of waiting, this one's for you.

Contents

Contents

Foreword

"I've always thought that giving forewords to a book required a certain kind of achievement in life, however, my childhood friend, Phidaribha, the author of this book, insisted that I should do it instead. Perhaps, having a friend like Ribha (a nickname I've been calling her since our childhood days) is one of my great achievements in life. She told me about the book a few months ago, however, she kept in mind that the whole idea of the book would be a surprise until the day it gets published. I've been respecting that decision ever since, however, I cannot deny the fact that my curiosity has been growing each day and I cannot wait to get my hands on the book. The reason why I am immensely excited to read Ribha's book is because of her personality, an intellectual with the kindest soul. I've known her for the longest time and I've always had this thought in mind that if she ever wrote a book, it would definitely be a good one and now she's actually doing it. I am a hundred percent positive that this book would empathise with many out there. I believe that she was given this purpose by our God Almighty and that it will impact each one of us in many different ways. I wish nothing but the best for her in her new journey as an author and I pray and hope that she writes more in the years to come."
- Felereen Adorisa Tariang
Author of Polaroid

Preface

Hailing from a small town in the North-East of India, Ribha is a graduate with a BA Hons in Economics from St.Mary's College, Shillong, Meghalaya.

Most of the instances recorded in this book really occured.

My book is intended to try to remind readers to overcome the stigma of mental illness by modeling love and acceptance.

'Don't let the fear of being labeled with a mental illness prevent you from seeking help. Don't let stigma create self-doubt and shame.'

Acknowledgements

To the people who are responsible for my existence - mom & dad, thank you for seeing me for the fullness of who I am - and like me. You never try to change me or mold me into your image. You've always listened well and delighted in me.

Prologue

'She lost him but found herself and somehow that was everything.'

Every choice you make is creating your future.

Choose yourself even if others refuse to.

Find the courage to let go of what you can't change.

CHAPTER ONE

"Maybe we are soulmates, but just met at the wrong time."

In 2011, Benjamin "Ben", a fifteen-year-old boy, sees thirteen-year-old Peyton at church, persues her, and they have a summer romance.

Ben comes from a humble background and becomes head over heels in love with Peyton, the grand-daughter of a rich elite family in Shillong, a hillstation in northeast India and capital of the state of Meghalaya.

Peyton's father, however, disapproves of Ben's feelings towards his daughter, due to his low social status. Despite this, Ben and Peyton, grow closer until Peyton's father sends her abroad for school.

CHAPTER TWO

"Some people lose diamonds in search of stones."

Peyton goes to Ben's house to spend one last day together. On their last day, they both make a promise that they will continue their correspondence with letters.

Ben and Peyton continue their relationship through letters. Their time apart started as weeks turned into months and years.

Peyton volunteers as a tutor in school for kindergarden students, where she meets Ezra, a young teacher who comes from old money. After a few years together, Peyton and Ezra have developed feelings for one another.

While Peyton still loves Ben, she breaks up with him through one of their letters.

In a fit of rage, Ben burns all of Peyton's letters.

CHAPTER THREE

"All she wanted was for his name to be written in her destiny."

Years later, Ben receives a prestigious art scholarship and moves to Guwahati where he encounters Peyton again. By this time, Ben is in a relationship with Joanna, a successful model, but Peyton's feelings for Ben have not changed.

Ben visits Peyton at her hotel and learns that Peyton still loves him, she loves Ezra too but not in the same way she loves Ben - that is why she has broken up with Ezra.

Ben and Peyton are tempted to pick up where they left off years earlier, but do not go through with their felings.

CHAPTER FOUR

"I hope you find someone who isn't confused about how they feel about you."

Joanna ventured into pageantry where she went on to win the main title of Mega Miss Northeast. After winning this pageant, Ben calls and invites Peyton to a celebratory party held in honour of Joanna. Peyton is petrified on getting the invitation.

One day before the celebratory party, Joanna stumbled upon George, her former lover, who wants to reconcile. Joanna decides to go with George as she is still in love with him.

CHAPTER FIVE

"Ladies, your career will never wake up one day and decide to leave you."

Ben and Peyton, both having lost their respective love interest(s), become friends to help one another through their loneliness.

Ben and Peyton become close. They find that the years haven't diminished the feelings they have for one another. But both resist love - Ben because he does not want to get his heart broken again and Peyton because she wants to concentrate on her studies.

Some days later, Peyton sees Ben with another girl. Heartbroken, she hangs out with multiple guys but doesn't happen to like any of them.

The next day, she informs Ben about an internship in Delhi and is leaving for three years, and bids him goodbye.

CHAPTER SIX

"If you had to choose between your boyfriend and your best friend, who would you choose?"

Arthur Jones is an economics student who lives in Shillong city with his widowed mother, brother Dan and sister Beth. He is extremely smart, however, his life is dull and overshadowed by the loss of his father until the arrival of Peyton who has joined the Department of economics in St.Anthony's College.

When Arthur meets Peyton for the first time, he is instantly smitten and Peyton too nurses a deep crush on him. They began dating and soon falling in love.

Peyton's best friend, Clara, also falls in love with Arthur but he constantly rejects her. Arthur reveals he is in love with Peyton instead.

Shockingly, Peyton leaves college mid-semester and loses contact with Arthur.

Clara and Arthur become close in college. Eventually, they bond and start falling in love.

A couple of months later, when Peyton returns to college, Clara and Arthur have entered into an official relationship. However, when Arthur glimpses Peyton, he is overwhelmed with memories and unresolved feelings for Peyton.

Arthur confesses to Clara his conflicting emotions about who he should be with and despite Clara saying that she still loves him inspite of everything, Arthur decides to return to Peyton only to witness Peyton and Ben embracing each other at a restaurant.

CHAPTER SEVEN

"I can stand him loving her."

Arthur realizes that he is not in love with Clara and breaks up with her. He asks Peyton to be with him instead. Peyton, however, explains that she has developed feelings for someone else because Peyton believes she has come in the way of Arthur and Clara being together. Peyton therefore takes up the task to reunite the two.

CHAPTER EIGHT

"When someone else's happiness is your happiness, that is love."

Peyton's mother confronts her what has happened. Peyton says she loves Arthur but has decided to hide it because she has a mental health condition, 'bipolar disorder'.

Peyton vows to bring Arthur and Clara together. She believes that Clara will be able to provide for him better than she can.

Peyton hatches a plan to transform Clara and Arthur's bond and gradually their friendship blossoms into love.

Clara and Arthur, the two rekindle their relationship.

CHAPTER NINE

"Destigmatize mental illness, build support for people with mental illnesses."

On New Year's Eve, Peyton has an episode of psychosis and is admitted to the hospital.

At the hospital, she regains consciousness but has lost all memories of the past few weeks and months.

Meanwhile, Arthur encounters Ben at a grocery store. Ben reveals the truth about Peyton and her mental health condition. When Arthur learns about this, he visits Peyton at the hospital. However, Peyton fails to recognize him.

Peyton is extremely confused and does not understand why she has left Ben and why Ben has not come to visit her.

"Appreciate your parents, you never know what sacrifices they went through for you."

Peyton's parents insist on taking her home but the doctors do not allow them to take her home yet.

Peyton is still extremely confused. Her doctors have attempted to help her regain her lost memory but Peyton is more driven to learn why Ben has not come to visit her not knowing that they have broken up years earlier.

CHAPTER ELEVEN

"Dare to live by letting go."

Arthur makes the choice to return to Clara.

On the other hand, Peyton is welcomed home with a surprise party by her relatives, but she finds it overwhelming and is still extremely confused.

Peyton's sister informs Ben about Peyton's desire to see him and therefore invites Ben to the surprise party but Ben declines the invitation. He reconciles with Joanna instead.

Peyton realizes her place in Ben's life and decides to leave the past behind her.

Soon, Peyton's life is stable once again.

Perfect Timing

How many times has He said it but I didn't listen?

Instead I rush forward so full of self-confidence without even a tiny bit of the fear of God.

Meanwhile, the Lord tells me :

"Wait upon me. You are my child. Trust in my timing and my plans. I will show you healing, liberation and miracles. Trust in Me.

Remember how I rose again on the third day.

I am the Lord your God."

- So I'll wait. I'll wait upon the Glory of God.

Because losing things does not always mean missing out.